Sarah A. Maher graduated from NYU and has a Graphic Design Certificate from Baruch. Sarah is the author of *Colors of the City*. This is her second book with Austin Macauley Publishers.

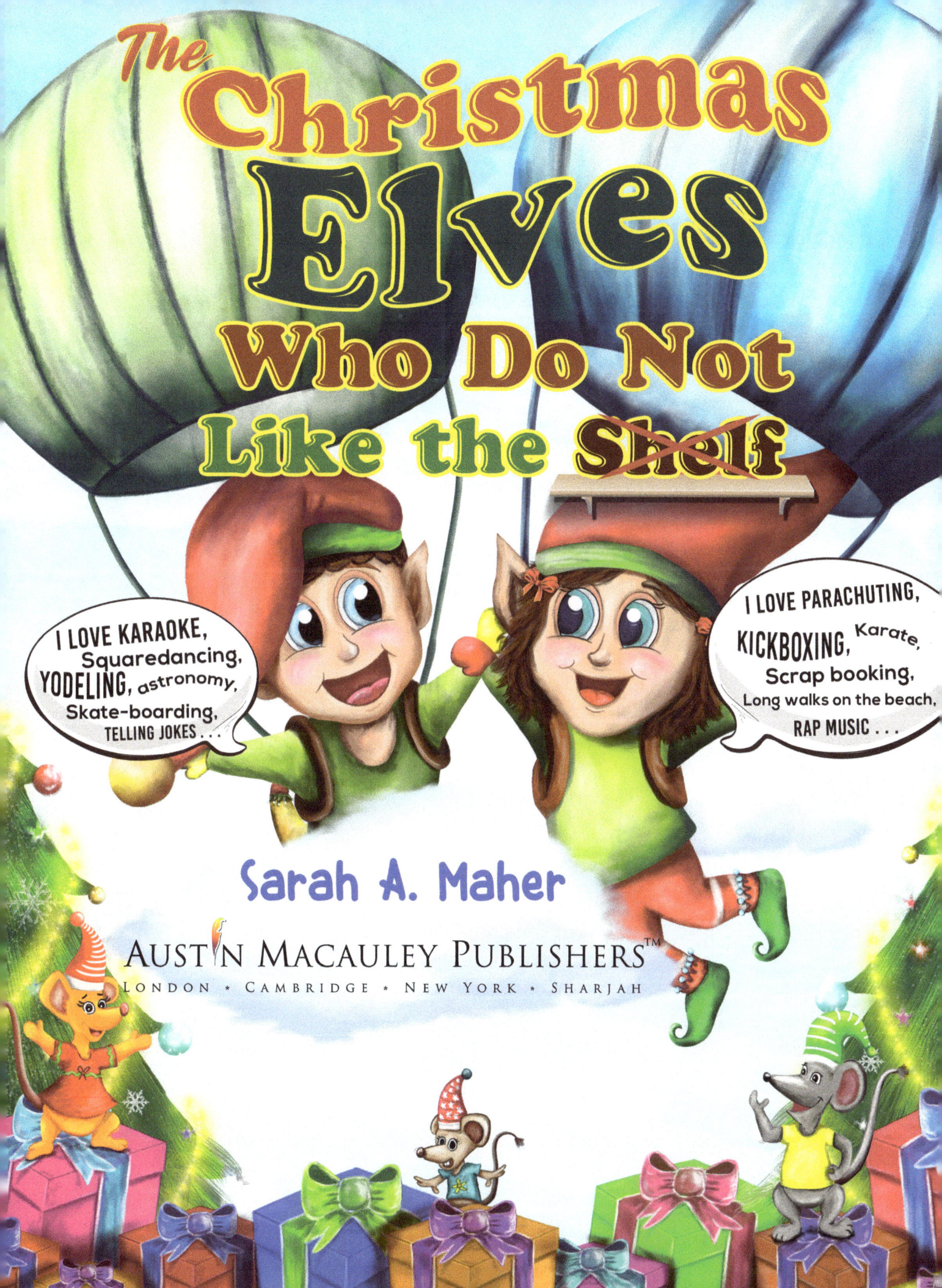

# Copyright © Sarah A. Maher (2019)

**Ordering Information:**
Quantity sales: special discounts are available on quantity purchases by corporations, associations, and others. For details, contact the publisher at the address below.

**Publisher's Cataloging-in-Publication data**
Maher, Sarah A.
The Christmas Elves Who Do Not Like the Shelf

ISBN 9781641828901 (Paperback)
ISBN 9781641828918 (Hardback)
ISBN 9781645366331 (ePub e-book)
Library of Congress Control Number:  2019914975

The main category of the book — JUVENILE FICTION / Holidays & Celebrations / Christmas & Advent

www.austinmacauley.com/us

First Published (2019)
Austin Macauley Publishers LLC
40 Wall Street, 28th Floor
New York, NY 10005
USA

mail-usa@austinmacauley.com
+1 (646) 5125767

I dedicate this book to my children:
Abigail, Liam, Caitlin, Francis Ronan, and James.

Also, to my father—forever in my heart—and mother, who always
made Christmases magical.

Hello... Hello... Hello!
My name is Randy, and this is Candy.
We do ~~not~~ like the ~~shelf~~!
We are not those kinds of elves.

We love to go to the
city to see the lights,
not sit on the shelf and see no sights.

At the Zoo, it's fun
to see the monkeys, lions, and kangaroos,
not on the shelf, singing the blues.

We love playing music in different bands,
heavy metal too,
not on the shelf looking
at our hands, thank you!

Next stop is London to see the Queen,
not on the shelf with no royalty.

We also love to skateboard fast,
not sitting on the shelf
like Christmases past.

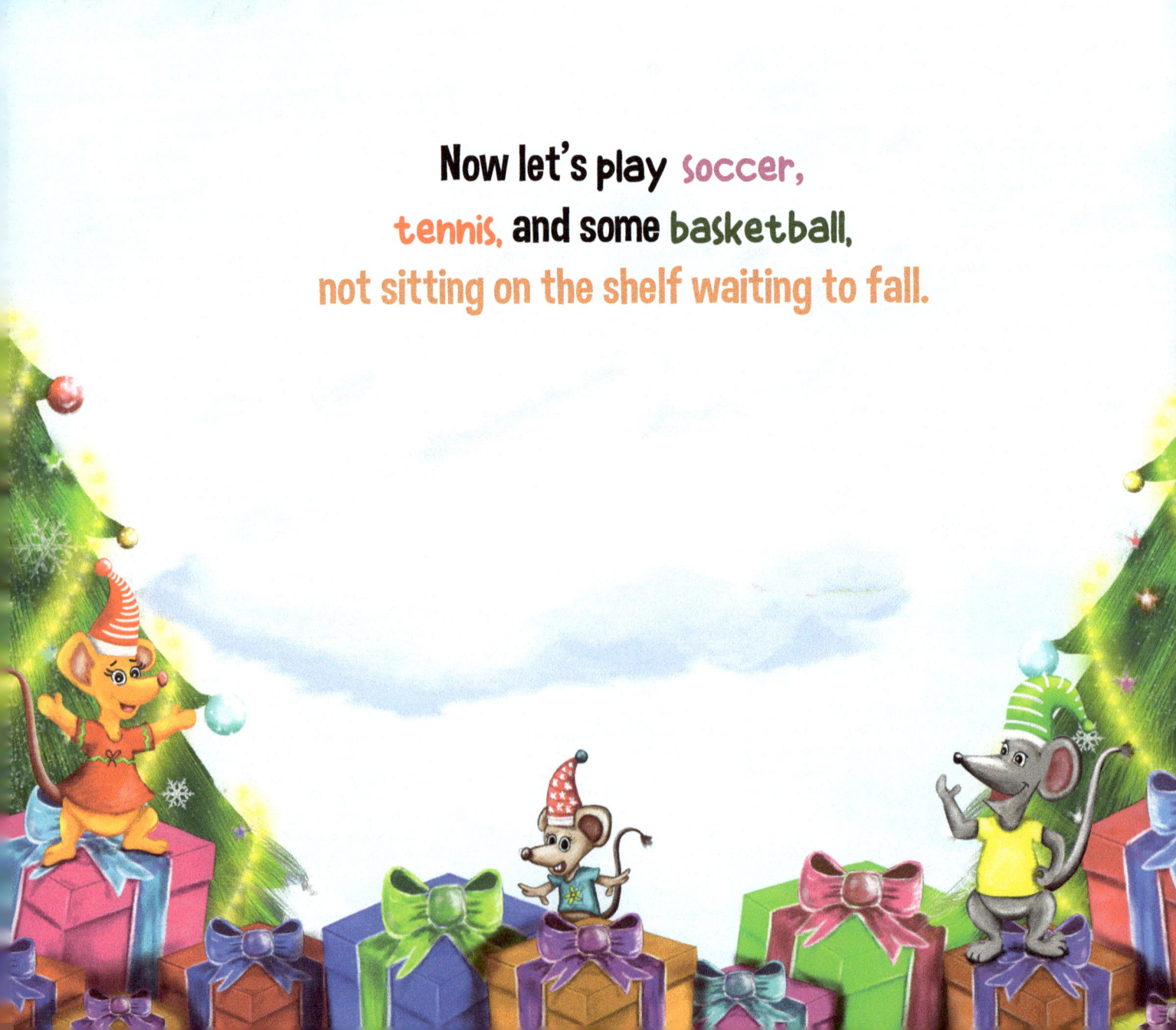

Now let's play soccer,
tennis, and some basketball,
not sitting on the shelf waiting to fall.

Here we go to the ranch
to see a cow or two,
not on the shelf, never hearing a moo-moo.

We especially like skydiving and
singing Christmas tunes, both at the same time,
not sitting on the shelf, bored out of our mind.

Then onto the desert to see the Pharisees,
not on the shelf watching temper tantrums, please!

Next let's take a trip to the islands and feel the sand,
not sitting on a wooden shelf, but on beautiful land!

Back at home we can jump in the
water and splash,
instead of sitting on the shelf
getting butt rash.

Let's go sailing and
fishing on the Ocean Blue,
instead of sitting on the shelf
with nothing to do.

We love to do karaoke and tell lots of jokes,
but if they are bad, we need to
say sorry to those folks.

We also love fighting with swords, not on the shelf looking at people give gifts they cannot afford.

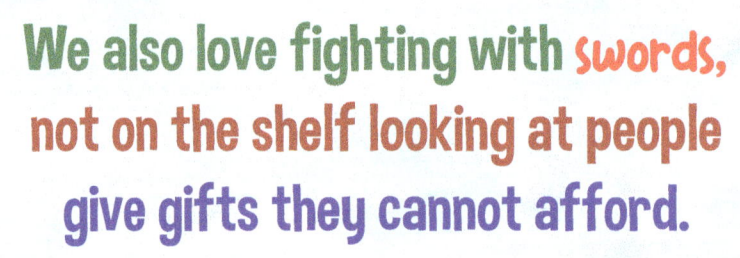

So as you can see,
we are adventurous elves,
we like to have fun,
instead of sitting on the shelf
and having none.

Thank you for coming along to hear
our story. One important thing, you cannot forget,
we do report back to Santa while having fun
and before the day is done.

So always be good little girls and boys,
so you can get lots of toys and joy.